This was the moment Judi had been waiting for, but she hadn't planned on her reaction. She'd never known such bone-chilling terror. Her mouth was dry. She wanted to scream, but no sound came out of her tight, parched throat.

A figure appeared at the entrance, but the door closed again too quickly for Judi to make out who, or what, it was. Darkness once more enveloped the room.

PROGRAMMED for TERROR

CAROL H. BEHRMAN

For Joe,
who can tame the ghost in any computer,
and Jeni,
who enjoys a good mystery

Published by Willowisp Press
801 94th Avenue North, St. Petersburg, Florida 33702

Copyright © 1994 by Willowisp Press,
a division of PAGES, Inc.

Printed in the United States of America

2 4 6 8 10 9 7 5 3

ISBN 0-87406-711-1

One

THE computers stood like space-age soldiers: five rows, four computers in each row.

Judi Newman sat at the first computer in the second row, directly in front of the teacher's desk. This was both good and bad. It was bad because she felt Mr. Pascal was watching her all the time. That made her nervous and fidgety. Sometimes it was hard to concentrate knowing that the teacher's cold gray eyes were on her.

On the other hand, Mr. Pascal was always right there to help whenever she was having trouble. It often seemed that the computer had a mind of its own and refused to do what Judi wanted, even when she was positive that she was pushing the right keys. But the computer always obeyed Mr. Pascal.

Everybody obeyed Mr. Pascal!

"Only three minutes left," announced Mr. Pascal, glancing at the big clock on the front wall. "You'd better start saving what you've done today."

Judi slipped the diskette labeled with her name into the drive. She began to follow the directions on the screen for SAVE. More than anything, she hoped she would be able to get it right. Last time, she had become hopelessly mixed up. Then she was totally humiliated when Mr. Pascal came up to her, fiddled rapidly on her keyboard, and said impatiently, "See how simple it is!"

This time, Judi worked slowly and carefully. She was rewarded when the magic words FILE SAVED flashed on the screen. Judi breathed a sign of relief.

"I hate computer class, don't you?" asked Shannon, Judi's friend, as they made their way down the hall toward the cafeteria after class. The next period was lunch, and it was none too soon for Judi. She was starving.

Judi glanced at her companion. Shannon was one of the tallest girls in seventh grade.

She was large-boned, too, and a real contrast to the thin, petite Judi. The two girls were sometimes the butt of comments from schoolmates: "Mutt and Jeff," "Fat and Skinny," and other brilliant observations. But Judi and Shannon were used to them. They had a lot of classes together, and had been best friends since kindergarten.

Judi shrugged. "At first I did hate computer class. But now that we're doing word processing, I like it a lot better."

Shannon skillfully elbowed a large boy who was trying to shove past her. "Mr. Pascal drives me up the wall," she said. "He thinks we should all be computer geniuses immediately, if not sooner."

The girls had arrived at the cafeteria. A crowd of noisy seventh graders was milling outside the closed door.

Judi nodded. "I know," she replied. "But now, I get so caught up in the story I'm writing that I don't mind Mr. Pascal as much as I did at first."

Shannon snorted and pushed her way through the crowd, forcing Judi to struggle along behind. "You've loved making up stories ever since we were little kids," Shannon said.

The door finally opened. A surge of impatient teenagers on the brink of starvation shoved Judi and Shannon into the cafeteria. The girls managed to get seats at the table they liked best, right next to the dessert line. They pulled out their sandwiches and continued their conversation.

"I especially like writing stories on the computer," said Judi. "It's great to be able to fix your mistakes and change stuff without having to write the whole thing over again."

Shannon nodded. "Rewriting is pretty bad," she agreed. "I'm not as good in English as you are, so I'm always having to do things over and over." Shannon bit heartily into her salami sandwich. "What kind of story are you writing, Judi?"

Judi grinned. "My favorite kind."

"Then it must be a ghost story," guessed Shannon.

Judi nodded.

"What's it about?" Shannon asked. Shannon was a good friend and a good fan— she always wanted to know about Judi's stories.

Judi bit into her sandwich and thought for a moment. She swallowed and said, "I don't know if I should tell you this time."

"Why not?" Shannon looked indignant.

"Well . . . ," Judi hesitated. "I was reading this article in one of Mom's magazines. It was about writers. It said that real writers never talk about their books until they finish them."

"That's dumb! Besides," Shannon pointed out, "you're not a real writer."

Something stirred within Judi. Something private and important. She ran her fingers through her curly brown hair. "I just don't feel like talking about it," Judi said.

"Oh, Judi! Please?" Shannon never gave up. Once she made up her mind to, Shannon could pull anything out of Judi.

"Well . . . I'll tell you this much. It's about a girl who's alone in her house on a dark, stormy night. Scary things happen."

"Like what?" Shannon had devoured her own lunch, and was eyeing the small bag of chocolate chip cookies that Judi was opening.

"That's all I'm telling," Judi declared. "Here. Have some." She pushed the cookies toward Shannon.

At that moment, the girls got a cookie they weren't expecting. A chunk of one sailed through the air. It glanced off Judi's head and landed on the table. They turned around quickly.

"It's that idiot, Jeff!" exclaimed Shannon.

Jeff Chapman, the self-appointed class clown, was sitting two tables away with a smirk on his freckled face. Shannon shook her fist at him. Judi twisted her face into as horrible an expression as she could muster. Jeff's grin just got wider. He broke off another piece of cookie.

"If he throws that at us," Shannon growled, "I'll break both his arms."

They were saved by a teacher who stopped at Jeff's table and ordered him to clean up all crumbs and cookie pieces. Shannon glanced at the clock and stuffed a cookie into her mouth. "That kid's lucky," she said. "I was ready to cream him."

Judi studied Jeff, who was busy brushing crumbs from the table. "I don't know why Jeff acts like such a jerk," she mused. "He's really not bad looking."

Shannon hooted. "Don't tell me you like Jeff?"

"Oh, no!" Judi assured her. "I was just wondering why he acts the way he does."

"Because he's stupid, that's why!"

Judi knew that Jeff wasn't stupid. But she didn't argue with her friend. After all, she wouldn't want anyone to think that she might like Jeff Chapman!

Lunch period was over before they knew it. The students marched to the door a lot slower than they had entered.

"Now," said Shannon, as they strolled to their lockers to pick up their books for afternoon classes, "tell me more about that ghost story."

Judi shook her head. She didn't want to talk about her story. Not yet, anyway. She turned to pick up a paper that had fallen out of her locker and came face to face with Jeff Chapman. Judi had the impression that he had been standing there watching her.

Jeff flushed. His face became so red that even his freckles faded.

"Oh . . . um . . . er . . . hi, Judi," he mumbled. Then he turned and fled down the hall.

Shannon was watching, her eyes bright with interest. "He likes you."

"Who?" asked Judi innocently.

"Jeff Chapman, who else? I bet he'd love to ask you out."

Judi laughed. "You've got to be kidding!"

"No, I mean it." Shannon gathered up her books.

"You'll never see me going out with Jeff Chapman," said Judi.

Shannon shrugged.

Judi stared down the hall where Jeff had disappeared. "What makes you think he likes me?"

Shannon grinned. "See? You *are* interested!"

"No, I'm not!" insisted Judi. "I was just wondering what gave you such a crazy idea."

"It's not crazy." Shannon nodded knowingly. "I've seen him looking at you in lunch and computer class. And it was you he was throwing cookies at. He likes you. I can tell."

Judi slammed her locker shut. "Well, I don't like him!" She began to stride down the hall.

Shannon caught up. "What will you say if he asks you to the seventh-grade dance?"

Judi squirmed. "I hate this conversation," she said. "Jeff Chapman is not going to ask me to the dance. And even if he did, I wouldn't go with him."

Shannon eyed Judi doubtfully. "Oh no?"

"No!"

"We'll see about that!" declared Shannon.

Judi shook her head. "Jeff's a nut," she insisted. But, she added to herself, he *is* sort of cute.

The next day, Judi sat in her second-period social studies class and tried hard to concentrate. She didn't have computer class until third period, but her mind kept wandering to her ghost story as Mrs. Grapple rambled on about the Civil War.

Instead of taking notes, Judi scribbled phrases for her story: *the howling wind, a shadowy figure in a dark corner,* and *something crashed in the attic.* Judi suspected she'd be in serious trouble when the time came to be tested on the Civil War. She made a valiant effort to listen and to note entries like *Battle of Bull Run* or *Sherman's March,* but inevitably her pen found other words: *The sound of marching feet in the dark basement. "Run, run, run," cried a voice in the dark.*

After class, Judi fell into step with Shannon in the corridor.

"Shannon, did you take notes today in social studies?"

"Sure. Grapple kills you if you don't," Shannon said.

"Could I borrow your notes tonight?" Judi asked.

Sharon immediately stopped, opened her notebook, pulled out two pages, and handed them to Judi. She didn't ask why Judi needed them. That's the sort of friend she was.

When they reached the computer room, Judi hurried to her work station. She was eager to get started, even though Mr. Pascal still made her a little nervous.

Not that Judi really believed all those stories about him—how he lived alone in a crumbling old house, how his basement was filled with odd electronic gadgets, and how he spent all his spare time fiddling with them, trying to invent something strange and freaky. Judi didn't care if he was some sort of weird, mad scientist like in the movies. She did care that in his class, Mr. Pascal expected everyone to understand how to use the computers without a hitch. Well, maybe some people could, but Judi wasn't one of them.

Judi sighed, then inserted her data disk, retrieved her story and scanned the monitor to review what she had written so far.

The first paragraph introduced a character named Judi (she always named her heroines after herself) and how she asked her parents not to go out because she didn't like being alone in the house on such a stormy evening. Her parents laughed at her fears and assured her they would be home early. In the second paragraph, the fictional Judi sat alone in the house and watched a movie on television.

Judi scanned her story and nodded with satisfaction. Then her eyes fell on the end of the last paragraph. She blinked once, twice, and drew her breath in.

"What's this?" she gasped.

Two

EVERYONE in class stopped working and stared at Judi. Mr. Pascal looked up from the papers he was correcting.

"Is there a problem, Judi?" Mr. Pascal's voice was clipped and precise. His pale, bland features betrayed no emotion.

"I didn't write this!" Judi said. She stared at the computer as if it were a two-headed monster.

"Did you take the wrong data disk?"

Judi looked at the monitor again. "No, this is my story."

"If that's your story," said the teacher dryly, "then you have the correct disk."

"But I didn't write the last part," said Judi.

Mr. Pascal got up and examined Judi's

monitor. "I don't see any problem here."

"Look at the last two sentences!" Judi pressed.

Mr. Pascal read them aloud: *A door creaked open mysteriously in the television movie. At the same time, an identical sound came from the rear of Judi's house.*

"I didn't write that," Judi insisted.

"Nonsense," said Mr. Pascal. "Of course you wrote it. There it is, right on the monitor."

Judi looked at the screen again. She remembered writing everything else that appeared there. But not those last two sentences. "No," she persisted. "I didn't write that."

Mr. Pascal gave Judi a half-smile and moved back to his desk. "You wrote it, Judi. You've just forgotten," he said.

Judi sighed. There was no point arguing with Mr. Pascal. Besides, he had to be right. No one else had access to her disk. She must have written those lines.

Judi read the words on the monitor again. Actually, she thought, those last two sentences were pretty good. And although she couldn't believe she'd think of something like that and not remember, she liked the lines anyway. Judi put her fingers on the keyboard and went on with the story.

Judi's eyes were wide with fright, she wrote. *Fearfully, she walked toward the back of the house. She peered through the kitchen door and turned on the light switch near the entrance. The kitchen was empty.*

The story took shape in Judi's mind as she tapped away on the keys. She was glad now that she had taken a typing course during the summer. It had seemed boring at the time. She'd rather have paddled around at the community pool. But now, it was so much faster to put her thoughts down. Judi watched the screen as her ideas transferred from her head to her fingers to the computer. The words flowed steadily as she became more and more involved in the story. Suddenly, Judi was astonished to hear Mr. Pascal's voice announce that the period was over. Computer class had never gone by so quickly! She was thrilled and delighted with her progress.

But later that afternoon, when Judi went to her locker to gather the books she needed for homework, she found her thoughts turning back to the strange occurrence in computer class. How could she have written those lines, and then forgotten about them?

A voice nearby snapped her back to the present. She glanced up to see Shannon eyeing her with curiosity.

"What was that all about in computers today?" asked Shannon.

Judi hesitated. Usually, she confided everything to her friend. But this was too weird. It made her look stupid. She shrugged. "It was nothing," she replied. "Just a problem I was having with the computer."

Shannon's eyebrows shot up, but for once she didn't push it. She grabbed her windbreaker. "Let's go to my house. My folks had company last night who brought over a two-pound box of chocolate-covered cherries."

Judi's eyes widened. "Chocolate-covered cherries?" She could almost feel that heavenly taste on her tongue. "I can't stand it! That's my favorite candy."

Computer class was forgotten for the moment.

But it came to mind again later that evening when the Newmans were eating dinner. Judi's dad, an engineer, began to talk about the computer at his office.

"I had to call in the programmers again,"

Mr. Newman complained as he sliced into his sirloin steak. "The third time this month. They keep sending over nincompoops who don't know how to program."

"What's *nincompoops*, Daddy?"

Judi's four-year old brother, Patrick, was always asking, "What does this mean?" and "What does that mean?" Judi's mom said it was a stage he was going through. Judi hoped her mom was right because if it went on much longer, she thought she might strangle the kid.

"It means stupid people," Judi told him, "like you."

Patrick began to cry, and Judi was scolded by her parents as usual. After the fuss had died down, Mr. Newman went on. "It's amazing. All that work we did on the Ferrier job was completely fouled up by that computer."

"What did the computer do, Dad?" Judi asked.

"It lost some of the info and mixed up other data so that what came out was different from what we had intended."

Judi put down her fork and stared at her dad intently. "A computer is able to change what you put into it?"

Judi's dad seemed pleased by her interest.

He tried to explain. "Yes and no. It can make changes—but only to the extent that it's programmed to. Our computer was supposed to be programmed to handle data in a certain way and it failed to do so."

"What's data?" asked Patrick, his mouth stuffed with mashed potatoes. No one paid any attention. Judi and her dad were intent on their conversation. Mrs. Newman was in the kitchen getting more rolls.

"But can the computer itself change or add to the data you put into it?" Judi persisted.

"What's data?" Patrick's voice rose.

"Are you talking about something specific, Judi?" her father asked.

Judi hesitated. She hadn't planned to say anything about what happened in her computer class. But her dad seemed to be describing a similar event. Maybe she hadn't imagined it after all. Maybe the computer really could put its own words into her story.

"Well, Dad," she began, glancing up as her mom returned, "I think that my computer at school might have done the same thing." She related what had happened.

"What's *pwogwam*?" Patrick demanded loudly.

Mr. Newman shook his head. "It's not the same thing at all, Judi," he told her. "The computer in my office failed because it wasn't programmed correctly. But you're using standard word-processing software. It won't print anything except what you put into it."

Patrick banged his spoon on the table. "What's *pwogwam?*"

"But Dad!" Judi insisted. "You just said that your computer changed things."

"That was the mistake of the *programmer,*" Mr. Newman explained. "The computer doesn't have a mind of its own. It only does what it's programmed to do. Your word-processing program is a standard one. It always works the same."

Patrick banged the table angrily. "What's *word pwocessing?* What's *pwogwam?*"

Mrs. Newman passed the steaming rolls. "Are you saying, dear, that Judi's teacher is right, that she must have written those sentences herself?"

Her husband nodded. "There's no other explanation."

Judi shook her head when the rolls came to her. She had lost her appetite. "But I didn't write them. I didn't! Why won't anybody believe me?"

"People do forget things," Mrs. Newman pointed out. She spoke loudly, trying to make herself heard above Patrick's table-thumping. "Why, only yesterday, I forgot to mention two important facts in a lesson on fractions, even though I've taught that lesson a hundred times." Judi's mom was a math teacher.

"What's a *faction?*" whined Patrick.

"I'm going to pound that kid!" Judi growled, turning to her little brother.

Patrick burst into tears. His parents moved quickly to comfort him.

"I'm going up to do my homework," muttered Judi. Her words were drowned out by her little brother's sobs, and her parents never even noticed her slip away.

Judi lay awake a long time after going to bed that night. By the time she fell into a troubled sleep, she was convinced that everyone else was right. She had written those lines herself. There was no other explanation.

Three

THE next day in computer class, Judi looked up to see Mr. Pascal watching her. There was a peculiar twist to his expression. Judi was beginning to wonder if all those rumors were true. Maybe he was a weirdo.

"What are you waiting for, Judi?" The teacher's voice was firm.

"I'm thinking."

"'Procrastinating' would be more accurate," Mr. Pascal remarked dryly.

Judi couldn't argue. He was right. She was doing exactly what he said—putting off getting started. With a sigh, she booted up the program, inserted her data disk into the drive, retrieved her file, and then faced the monitor expectantly. Her story flashed onto the monitor. Judi read it through from the start. Slowly, she moved the cursor down and brought new words onto the screen. She came to the end, and inhaled sharply.

It had happened again!

The previous day, Judi ended her story with her heroine asleep in front of the television.

But now there were two additional sentences: *Judi awoke with a start. A dark shape was coming toward her, and in its hand was a long, deadly knife.*

Judi stared at the screen. She had not written those words! She knew she hadn't!

"Is anything wrong, Judi?" Mr. Pascal stood at her side and looked over her shoulder at the screen.

Judi knew that she risked looking foolish again. But the words tumbled from her mouth. "It happened again!"

"It?" The teacher raised an eyebrow. "Exactly what is 'it'?"

"The computer," Judi said. Her eyes were fastened to the monitor. "It added something to my story again."

"Of course it did." Mr. Pascal's tone had a tinge of humor. "This computer is a regular Shakespeare."

Judi shrank into her chair. "I didn't write those last sentences," she said in a small voice.

Mr. Pascal examined the monitor and read the offending words aloud. "Of course you wrote it," he concluded. "It's written in the same style as the rest."

"But I *didn't*," Judi insisted. He must believe her. She was telling the truth.

Mr. Pascal didn't reply immediately. He returned to his chair and sat down. Picking up a pen, he began to tap it steadily on the desk, the rhythmic taps growing harder and louder each second. His eyes were fixed on Judi, as if examining her closely. Finally, he spoke.

"What's going on, Judi?"

"What do you mean?" Judi's heart beat faster. She felt a creeping sense of guilt.

The teacher stared at her warningly. "Don't think you can fool me," he said. The amusement had disappeared from his voice. "I know this is some sort of joke. Please understand that I don't appreciate it and I won't stand for it." He spoke softly, but the understated threat in his voice frightened Judi more than shouting. She trembled and couldn't speak.

And she didn't dare look around—she was convinced everyone was laughing at her.

"Did you hear what I said, Judi?" demanded the teacher.

Judi nodded helplessly.

"I don't want to hear that sort of nonsense again," Mr. Pascal ordered. "Is that clear?"

"Yes," whispered Judi, wishing that she could disappear and never have to face anyone ever again. For a moment, silence hung over the classroom.

Then the sound of clicking keys told Judi that the other students had returned to work. Mr. Pascal was called to a station at the rear to help someone in trouble, and Judi was mercifully released from his glare. She peeked back quickly, afraid that everyone was still looking at her. But no one was except Tom Gruber in the back row, who had a sly grin.

Judi's thoughts were in a jumble. Why wouldn't anyone believe her? She hadn't written those sentences—she knew she hadn't. But what other explanation was there? She remembered what her father had said: "The computer doesn't have a mind of its own. It only does what it's programmed to do."

Judi looked again at the words on the

screen: *Judi awoke with a start. A dark shape was coming toward her, and in its hand was a long, deadly knife.*

Judi didn't have anything like that in mind when she was writing the story. Yet there it was on the monitor—and she didn't like it at all. Suddenly she felt an urgent need to rescue her heroine from danger.

Judi slowly lifted her fingers to the keyboard and carefully deleted the terrible words. Then she began to type the story the way she wanted it. She continued without interruption until Mr. Pascal announced the period was almost over.

Judi turned off her computer and put her disk in the file box on Mr. Pascal's desk. She was careful to avoid looking at him or at anyone else. She slipped out of the room, hoping to escape before anyone could question her about what had happened.

Shannon caught up with her in the hall.

"Listen," she said, grabbing Judi's arm, "you'd better tell me what's going on." There was concern in her eyes.

"You wouldn't believe it, Shannon." Judi shook her head. "It's too crazy."

"Try me!"

Judi couldn't hold back the tears.

"Oh, Shannon!" she said miserably. "I don't know what's happening!"

A few moments later, seated at their favorite table in the lunchroom, Judi told her friend everything.

"There must be something wrong with me," she concluded weakly. "That's what everyone is thinking, and I guess everyone's right."

"That's stupid," Shannon assured her. "I know you better than anyone else, and I'm telling you right now there is nothing wrong with you."

Judi smiled gratefully. "Then what do you think is happening?" she asked as she pushed away a mostly uneaten peanut butter sandwich.

"That's obvious. Someone is playing a joke on you."

Judi shook her head. "I thought of that, too," she told Shannon. "But it isn't possible."

"Why not?"

"Nobody else can use my disk. Didn't you ever notice how Mr. Pascal takes the file box out of a locked cabinet at the beginning of each period, and locks it up again at the end?

There's no way anyone could get at my disk."

Sharon munched on a Twinkie. "You're right," she agreed. "I didn't think of that."

"So you see," Judi concluded, "there's only one possibility. I must be crazy." She looked around nervously, hoping that no one was listening. She was glad that she and Shannon were alone at the table, and for once, she was grateful for the noise in the cafeteria that drowned out what they were saying. Judi stuffed her sandwich back into the lunch bag. She started to get up to throw it away, but Shannon restrained her.

"Listen." Shannon looked her straight in the eye. "If there's one thing I know, it is that you are *not* crazy. There has to be some other explanation."

"Yeah? What?"

Shannon stroked her cheek thoughtfully. "Maybe you really did forget what you wrote. I mean, I'm working on a story, too. Every day when I get to class, I have to read the whole thing from the beginning because I don't remember what I wrote the day before."

"You don't?" asked Judi.

"Uh-uh!" Shannon shook her head. "It's just make-believe. So many more important things happen the rest of the day that the dumb story just leaves my mind."

"Do you think that's what happened to me?"

Shannon nodded. "I'm sure of it."

Judi sighed. "I don't know," she said doubtfully. "I was positive that I didn't write those last two sentences."

Shannon suddenly sat up straight, her eyes glowing. "I've got an idea!"

"What?" Judi asked hopefully.

"Do you remember exactly where you left off today?" Shannon asked.

Judi nodded. "Every word. I erased those awful sentences that didn't belong. What happens now is that the girl wakes up, turns off the television, and decides to go to bed. She's just finished changing into her pajamas when she hears someone on the stairs. The last words I wrote were *Judi opened her door just a crack and looked out into the hall.*"

"Okay." Shannon reached for her notebook, ripped out a page and handed it, together with a pencil, to her friend. "Write that down now, while it's still fresh in your mind. Then tomorrow, you'll know for sure whether anything new has been added."

Judi grabbed the pencil and began to write furiously. "You're a genius, Shannon. This is a great idea! Now I'll be able to prove that I'm not making this up."

Shannon watched Judi scribbling. "Or," she pointed out, "you'll see that what you're writing now will turn out to be the last words in the computer."

Judi hoped that Shannon was right and that the next day, when she went to computer class, she would see the same words on the screen that she had just put down on paper. Anything else was too weird to think about.

But Judi had a sinking feeling that was becoming eerily familiar.

Four

THE next morning, Judi woke with a terrible pain in her stomach. She tossed and turned and groaned, and her mom said she could stay home from school. Mrs. Newman took the day off to stay with her. She gave Judi some white, horrible-tasting medicine, fed her toast and herb tea, and let her stay in bed all day, reading and watching TV. By the late afternoon, the pain in her stomach was gone and she was starved.

"I think you'll be able to go to school tomorrow," said Mrs. Newman.

"Yeah," Judi replied without enthusiasm. Why couldn't she get some longer-lasting illness like the flu or chicken pox? Then she'd be able to stay in bed for a few days, even a week.

But the next day, Judi couldn't fake it, especially after devouring two large bowls of cereal topped with sliced bananas. So later that morning at school, she was once more face to face with the computer.

While her disk was loading, Judi looked up. Mr. Pascal was watching her. He gave a warning look.

He's waiting for me to make a fool of myself, thought Judi. Then a crazy idea came into her mind. What if Mr. Pascal was messing around with her story? Everyone said he was weird. And he *was* the only one who had access to all the disks.

Judi squeezed her eyes shut and tried to clear her head. She decided the theory was dumb. No teacher would do such a thing. Mr. Pascal probably wasn't even watching her. Even so, Judi vowed that no matter what came up on the computer, she would not give Mr. Pascal a reason for getting on her case again. She took a deep breath and looked at the monitor.

It was all she could do to stifle a scream. There on the monitor was her worst fear.

Not only had something new been added, but the last sentence Judi had deleted was back. The last part of her story read: *Judi opened her door just a crack and looked out into the hall. A dark shape was coming toward her, and in its hand was a long, deadly knife. Judi stared in horror, unable to move. The huge figure came closer, stood over Judi and slowly brought down the murderous blade.*

Judi knew that she had not written those lines. She reached into her notebook and pulled out the paper that spelled out the last words she had written two days before. She looked at them carefully, then at the screen.

The words on her computer screen weren't hers. She held the proof in her hand. Someone was interfering with her story.

But who would or could do such a thing?

Even worse—if not who, then what?

And why?

"How's it coming along, Judi?"

Judi jumped. Mr. Pascal was standing over her, peering at the monitor. He nodded. "Looks like an exciting story. Are you having any more problems with the computer?"

Judi wanted to shriek, "Yes, yes, yes!" But all she managed to do was shake her head. She didn't trust herself to speak.

Mr. Pascal didn't seem to notice Judi's

agitation. He was still looking at the screen. "That girl's in a bad spot," he commented, in an amused voice. "I hope she's not going to die horribly."

Judi didn't dare look up. There was no way she could keep the doubt from showing in her eyes. She shrugged and let her fingers strike the keyboard anywhere just to pretend everything was okay and she was going on with the story. To her relief, Mr. Pascal moved on to the student behind Judi.

But the teacher's comment only increased Judi's anxiety. *"I hope she's not going to die horribly."* Why would Mr. Pascal say such a thing? Why did he stare at her in such a knowing way?

Suddenly, a new, even more dreadful thought occurred to her.

Could this be some sort of threat? The girl in the story was also named Judi. If the fictional Judi were to die, would that mean that the real Judi . . . ?

Judi shook her head. She just couldn't think straight. It wasn't until she heard Mr. Pascal's voice announcing the end of the period that she realized she hadn't done a thing except stare at the computer. Was there some evil force in it? Was that possible? *Could the computer itself have power to harm her?*

Despite the panic she felt rising, there was one important thing Judi knew she had to do before she left. Hurriedly, she deleted the unwanted portion of the story and ejected her disk. Then she lay the disk in the box on the teacher's desk. But at the door, she lingered for a moment to watch Mr. Pascal close the box, unlock the cabinet, place the box inside, and lock it carefully once again. As ordinary as it seemed, his routine only increased Judi's terror.

How could this be happening?

By the time Judi arrived at the lunchroom, Shannon was already eating. Judi rushed over to their table. Before she even sat down, she poured out the latest news.

"The computer did it again!" Judi exploded. "It changed my story." She held up the paper Shannon had torn from her notebook, and waved it at her friend. "Remember this?" Judi said. "You were right, Shannon. This *is* proof. There was a completely different addition to the story when I booted up my disk today."

Shannon munched on a handful of potato chips, her expression thoughtful.

"Well?" demanded Judi. "How could this be happening?"

Shannon shrugged. "It's weird," she finally said. "I don't know what to say."

"I'll tell you what I think," said Judi. "I think that computer is trying to kill me."

"Oh, Judi!" Sharon began. "I don't—" She was interrupted by the appearance of a husky blond boy.

"Can I talk to you a minute, Shannon?"

"Sure, Jimmy."

Judi glared at Jimmy Bannister. Why did he have to bust in on them when they were having such an important conversation? She listened impatiently as Jimmy asked Shannon if she would go with him to the seventh-grade dance.

Who cares about a dumb dance at a time like this, Judi thought. To her disgust, Shannon was suddenly all smiles, and she tossed her long hair as she accepted the invitation. Jimmy hung around for what seemed like an eternity to Judi. Finally, he strutted back to his own table.

"Thank goodness he's gone!" said Judi. She turned eagerly to her friend. "Shannon, you've got to help me. I—"

"Can you believe it, Judi?" Shannon's voice

registered excitement. "I'm going to the dance with Jimmy Bannister! I never thought he would ask me."

"That's great, Shannon." Judi tried to sound enthusiastic, but her own problem took priority. "Do you think there's some supernatural force at work?"

"What?" Shannon eyes were sparkling. Even her skin seemed to glow. "Oh, you mean that business with the computer? Uh, I suppose it could be something like that. But, listen Judi, did you see what just happened? Jimmy Bannister asked me to the dance! Isn't it awesome?"

"Shannon!" Judi couldn't believe what she was hearing. "How can you think about a dance when my life is being threatened?"

"I'm sorry," said Shannon. "But I'm so excited. I can't think about anything else right now. Oh, Judi! We're going to have so much fun. I know someone will ask you, too."

"Oh yeah? Who?" Judi was becoming interested in spite of herself.

Shannon looked around the room. "Jeff Chapman, that's who. He's always staring at you. I'm sure he's going to ask you to the dance."

Judi looked at Jeff Chapman's table. Jeff's back was to her. "He is not staring at me."

"Well, he was a minute ago," Shannon said.

Judi wondered about Jeff. But Shannon was usually right about these things. Maybe he will ask me to the dance, Judi thought. Then again, he probably won't.

"I wouldn't go with him anyway," she said.

"Oh no?" Shannon grinned. "You'd jump at the chance, and you know it."

"Well," Judi admitted, "it would be better than going alone."

"It'll be great, Judi. We can go shopping together for our dresses."

Judi was about to say that she might no longer be among the living by the night of the dance, but a teacher came by and told the girls it was time to leave.

The rest of that day, Shannon went on and on about her dress, how she should get her hair styled, Jimmy Bannister's eyes, and Jimmy Bannister's cute blond hair. The dance was now at the top of Shannon's list of important topics. Judi's computer problems had dropped to a place near the bottom. When Judi tried to talk about her fears, Shannon dismissed them with, "Oh, someone's playing a stupid joke on you," and that was the end of it.

Later, Shannon suggested that Judi come to her house after school. Judi made up an excuse about having to help her mom. She didn't want to hear another word about the dance. Before today, it would have been as important to Judi as it was to Shannon. Now it seemed trivial to worry about a dance and who might or might not invite her, when it seemed like she was in danger.

Judi wanted to be alone to sort out the confusing events that were starting to control her life.

All that afternoon and evening, Judi stayed in her room. She pretended to do homework while she searched for a solution to her dilemma. But she couldn't come up with an explanation that made sense. Judi may have erased those awful words from her story, but they burned in her mind: *The huge figure came closer, stood over Judi, and slowly brought down the murderous blade.*

At dinner that evening, Judi asked her dad whether his computer was still misbehaving.

Mr. Newman told her that all was well. "I think these programmers finally got out all the kinks." He smiled reassuringly while passing the peas. "And your computer at school?" he inquired. "I trust that it has given up trying to compose its own stories."

Judi hesitated. She wanted to tell her parents what happened, but some instinct told her that their reactions would mirror Mr. Pascal's. They might think she was crazy and get all upset, and even send her to see someone.

She certainly didn't want to share her story with some nosy woman like Mrs. Abrahams, a school counselor who also happened to be a psychologist. Judi had seen Mrs. Abrahams around school. She wasn't the sort of person who would believe a tale about haunted computers.

So Judi just smiled and changed the subject. She even managed to control her temper when Patrick spilled his milk all over her new cotton skirt.

But later that night, Judi almost confided her fears to her mom. Judi was getting ready for bed when her mom knocked on the door and came in.

"Are you feeling better?" she asked.

"Yes."

"No more stomachache?" Mrs. Newman's eyes reflected concern.

Judi shook her head. "I'm okay."

"Are you sure?" Mrs. Newman persisted.

"Really, I'm fine now," Judi assured her.

Mrs. Newman sat at the edge of the bed and motioned for Judi to sit beside her. She put an arm around Judi. "Are you having any problems at school, dear?"

Judi could feel her eyes grow moist and knew tears were not far behind. "I'm having trouble in computers," she admitted.

Mrs. Newman patted her softly. "There's nothing to worry about," she said in a soothing voice. "Many of the kids at my school find it difficult to understand that subject at first."

"It isn't that, Mom. It's . . . " Judi dabbed at her eyes and turned to face her mother. "Mom, if one of your students was acting weird, what would you do?"

"Why, I'd talk to him and try to find out the problem. If the unusual behavior persisted, I'd have a conference with the parents and perhaps consult the school psychologist."

Judi stiffened. That was it! She knew it! If she told any of the adults what was happening, they'd call everyone in and make a federal case of it. She could see them now, her parents, teachers, the principal, the psychologist—all hovering over her with solemn, worried faces, asking questions, making her take piles of clever tests to prove she was crazy.

Judi wasn't about to let that happen. She dried her eyes quickly and assured her mom that everything would be okay once she mastered the computer. Then she went to bed and lay awake a long time, thinking.

The evil presence in the computer was her problem, and hers alone. She had to figure out a way to deal with it by herself. No one else would—or could—help her. She had to find an answer. And soon.

Five

THE days rolled by, each like a waking nightmare. Every morning, Judi found it harder to go to school than the day before. She could picture the computer waiting for her, and trembled when Mr. Pascal's class rolled around. And each day, her fears were more fully realized.

No matter how many times she deleted threatening words, the next day they would appear again in a different place. And they'd be followed by some new, ghastly addition. Judi erased the part about a figure with a knife at the bedroom door, and instead made her heroine look out in the hall and see nothing. The next time Judi booted up the story, the murderous shape with its ever-present knife was coming in through an open window. Judi deleted that and had the fictional Judi close the window. The following day, the monster was pounding at the bedroom door.

Just sitting down at her work station made Judi's stomach turn. The machine glowed at her like an alien. The monitor was a green, unblinking face. The disk drive was a mouth ready to spew grim threats.

Judi told no one but Shannon about how bad things really were. What was the use? No one would believe her. At least Shannon knew she was telling the truth, and was sympathetic. They'd been friends for so long, Shannon always knew when Judi was unhappy. Shannon even stopped planning for the dance long enough to come up with some new ideas.

"Maybe you could drop computer class," she suggested one day.

"You know I can't do that," Judi responded. "Computer class is required in seventh grade."

"Why don't you delete the *whole* story and start again?"

Judi smiled grimly. "I thought of that. Yesterday, I began a completely new story. It's not a ghost story. In fact, it's supposed to be funny. But when I looked at it today, the ending had been changed in a way to turn it into a scary story again."

Shannon shook her head. "I just can't believe a computer did that."

"I know it's hard to believe," agreed Judi, "but what other explanation is there?"

"I'll ask Jimmy about it," Shannon offered. "He's a whiz at computers."

"Don't you dare!" Shannon's words threw Judi into a panic. "He'll tell the other kids and I'll be the laughingstock of the whole seventh grade.

"Okay! Okay!" Shannon said quickly. "I won't say a word."

"Do you swear it?"

"Sure." Introducing Jimmy Bannister into the conversation set Shannon off again on the subject of the dance. "It's coming up pretty soon," she told Judi. "When are we going shopping for our dresses?"

"I'm not going to the dance," muttered Judi.

Much as she tried, the seventh-grade dance just wouldn't stick in her mind as important. Instead, she zeroed in on something Shannon had said.

Jimmy Bannister. A computer whiz? Wouldn't a computer whiz know how to mess up a computer and get it to do weird things? Jimmy wasn't in Judi's computer class. He was in Mr. Pascal's *last* period class. Wouldn't that give him a perfect opportunity to hang around after school and mess with the computers? But why would Jimmy do such a thing to her? Why would anyone?

Shannon's voice interrupted Judi's thoughts. "Of course you're going! I can't believe Jeff Chapman hasn't even hinted at it to you yet."

"I told you, Jeff Chapman doesn't know I exist. Besides, he's such a show-off. I wouldn't go with him even if he asked." Judi half-believed what she was saying. But only half.

Shannon grinned. "You're wrong. Jeff does too know that you exist."

"Well, the dance is coming up soon, and he hasn't said a word about it," said Judi.

"He will," Shannon assured her. "And if he doesn't, someone else will." Her expression grew thoughtful. It was a look that Judi knew well.

"You're planning something, Shannon. I can tell."

"Who, me?" Shannon smiled sweetly.

* * * * *

The following day, Tom Gruber came over to Judi during study period. He was cute, laid-back, and really fun-loving. Everyone liked Tom. Judi liked him, too, in a casual, friendly way. She just wished he were taller. Even Judi was taller than Tom, and she was one of the smallest kids in seventh grade.

"Hi, Judi."

"Hi." Judi put down her book and looked at him quizzically. What could he want? Maybe he needed help with Language Arts homework. Judi was good in that subject, and kids sometimes came to her with questions. Maybe it was something about computers. Tom was in Judy's class. She sometimes caught him looking at her. Judi had the feeling he liked her. He wasn't her type, but it was nice to be admired.

Tom came right to the point. "Are you going to the dance?"

Judi hadn't been expecting that question. "Uh, no, I mean, I don't know."

"How about going with me?"

"Okay." That wasn't what Judi had planned to say. Somehow, it just slipped out.

"Great! I'll talk to you later about the time and all." Tom looked relieved and went back to his seat. Judi watched as he and Jimmy Bannister began to whisper together.

Jimmy Bannister! That was it!

Judi turned to Shannon, who had been watching her with uncharacteristic silence. "You did this!" Judi said. "You spoke to Jimmy and he got Tom to ask me to the dance!"

Shannon shrugged. "Maybe I did and maybe I didn't. Anyway, now you're going, and we can shop for our dresses tomorrow. Won't that be great?"

All of a sudden, it did seem great. Judi was going to the dance! She'd rather have gone with Jeff Chapman, but he wasn't going to ask her.

Suddenly, a disturbing thought struck Judi. Could Tom be the one who was changing the stories on her computer? Maybe he and Jimmy were in it together. But Judi pushed the idea away. There was no way anyone could get her disk without a key. Besides, Tom was nice and could be lots of fun. She and Tom would hang around with Shannon and Jimmy and have a great time at the dance.

For the first time in days, the computer was almost forgotten, and Judi felt like anyone else.

"I know just what I want," she told Shannon. "A white dress with a wide pleated skirt. I saw one like it at Macy's a few weeks ago." The girls began to talk about dresses, shoes, and accessories. They made plans to shop the next afternoon.

For the rest of that day, whenever dark thoughts intruded, Judi managed to block them by concentrating on the dance. She was in such a good mood that after school, she invited her brother Patrick into her room and lavished him with patience and affection. She'd been short-tempered with him recently, and made up for it by playing his favorite games.

Patrick was so grateful that he flung his chubby arms around her. "I wuv you, Judi."

Judi hugged him tightly. This was better than fighting all the time. Why had she been so mean to her little brother? It was all that rotten computer's fault! If she could only figure out what was going on, everything would be okay.

She hated it. She hated that computer!

Suddenly, Judi realized what she was doing. She was hating a machine. A stupid machine! Judi began to laugh. Patrick laughed, too, even though he hadn't the slightest idea what he was laughing about.

I'll think about the dance instead, Judi decided. She pictured herself whirling in a pretty white dress and felt so good that she even offered to help her mom with dinner. Judi told her about the dance, and got permission to go shopping with Shannon the next day.

"I'll pick the two of you up at school," Mrs. Newman offered. She looked fondly at her daughter. "I'm glad to see you in such a good mood, Judi. You've seemed kind of blue lately." She gave Judi a quick kiss. "You'll have a terrific time at the dance."

Judi realized that her mother thought she had been unhappy because she was afraid no one would ask her to the dance.

Well, let her believe that, Judi decided. It made a lot more sense than a haunted computer. Besides, maybe there was some truth in her mother's explanation of her foul mood. Maybe deep down she'd been more upset than she realized when Shannon got an invitation and she didn't.

That night, before falling asleep, Judi focused on dresses and lively music instead of scary computers. She felt more in control than she had in a long time.

But the next day at school, the computer had a message for Judi even worse than any of the others: *A horrible, ghostly voice seemed to come from every part of the house. "We will let you live a few more days," the voices whispered. "But on the night of the dance, you will surely die."*

Judi's high hopes crashed instantly, replaced with a familiar dread.

This was a threat. There was no doubt about it. Somebody or something knew Judi's every move. If there was an evil entity in the computer that meant to scare the daylights out of her, well, it was doing a good job. Would it be just as efficient when it came to murder?

"Isn't this a bit extreme, Judi?"

Judi jumped. She hadn't seen Mr. Pascal standing behind her reading her monitor.

"I didn't write that!" Judi exclaimed without thinking.

"What did you say?" The teacher's voice was sharp.

Judi managed to regain her self control.

"What I mean is, that isn't what I meant to write. I'm going to change it right now."

Without daring to look at Mr. Pascal, Judi deleted the offending words. She replaced them with the only thing that came to mind: *Judi heard her parents come in, and was relieved to know that she was safe at last.*

"That's a lot better," said Mr. Pascal, returning to his desk. But when Judi happened to glance up, she found him looking at her.

He didn't believe her, Judi realized. He thought she was a weird kid.

He'll be sorry when I'm dead.

The horrible thought came unbidden into Judi's mind. Then he'll know I was telling the truth, she thought bitterly. They'll all believe me then. But it'll be too late.

Judi stared at her monitor. She didn't like what she had written about the girl's parents coming home. What kind of story was that? A boring story, that's what it was. It was boring and she hated it. She liked excitement in her writing. Scary stuff, too. But this computer added such horrible scenes to the story that it was more than scary—it was threatening. Judi had no idea what to write next.

Besides, did it really matter what she wrote? By tomorrow, her computer would only change it to a new threat. So Judi wrote something stupid about the girl telling her parents all about the scary things that went on while they were gone. The parents insisted that it had just been the girl's imagination. Isn't that what adults always said?

The computer period seemed to last forever. Not so long ago she had loved working on this story. Judi sighed with relief when the class finally came to an end. She read what she had written while the computer was saving the new work on her disk. It was as dull as mud.

"See what you can do with that!" Judi muttered. As she took out her disk, she saw Mr. Pascal staring at her, a peculiar expression on his face.

Now he's sure I'm strange, Judi thought. She wanted to punch the computer, to beat it into behaving right. She got up quickly—too quickly. Her sleeve caught on the edge of the keyboard. She lost her balance, tripped over the chair and landed with a thud on the floor.

Humiliated, Judi scrambled to her feet. She heard some kids laughing, but it didn't seem important for long. All she could think about was the computer and the awful power it had—power that increased daily.

It's actually starting to hurt me now, Judi thought. She gingerly touched a sore spot on her wrist.

What will it do next?

Six

THE sign on the door of Room 203 read MRS. LEONA ABRAHAMS, SCHOOL COUNSELOR.

What am I *doing* here, Judi wondered. Someone had delivered a note to the teacher in Judi's last period class. The teacher took Judi aside and told her to go Mrs. Abraham's office right away.

Judi was scared. She'd spoken to school counselors before, but never to one who was also a psychologist. Would Mrs. Abrahams be able to see right through her?

Timidly, Judi turned the knob and pushed the door open. She walked into a bright, cheerful room with white walls and several large, brightly colored framed posters. Toys and games were neatly piled on a table near the door.

"You must be Judi." The woman seated behind the large desk didn't look scary. In fact, she looked like Judi's grandmother. Her dark eyes were gentle and compassionate. She smiled warmly and pointed to a yellow plastic chair opposite the desk.

"Sit down, dear."

Judi sat down warily. In spite of Mrs. Abrahams' grandmotherly appearance, Judi was on guard. She tried to empty her mind and look innocent.

"Do you know why you're here?" Mrs. Abrahams asked.

Judi shook her head. She didn't want to speak if she could avoid it. Her voice might give her away.

"Some people who care about you are concerned that you seem to be unhappy lately."

Judi hated phoniness.

"It's not *some* people!" she burst out. "It's Mr. Pascal, isn't it?"

Mrs. Abrahams shook her head. "Not just Mr. Pascal. Your other teachers have also noted a change in you recently. And I've also been in touch with your parents. They're concerned, too, and agreed it might be a good idea for me to talk to you."

"They did?" Judi didn't realize that her problems were so obvious.

"Would you like to talk about it?" Mrs. Abrahams' eyes were gentle and understanding.

Judi shook her head. No way! She wasn't going to be tricked into admitting there was something wrong with her. Especially when it wasn't true.

Mrs. Abrahams leaned back in her chair. "What you say in this room is confidential," she assured Judi. "Often, when something bothers us, it really does help to talk about it."

"I *have* tried to talk about it," Judi protested. "But no one will believe me except Shannon."

"Shannon?"

"My best friend. She knows I'm telling the truth."

"The truth about what?"

Judi hesitated. Could she trust this woman? It would be such a relief to share her problem with someone other than Shannon. All Shannon could talk about lately about was the dance. Maybe Mrs. Abrahams would understand. After all, she was a psychologist.

"It's my computer," Judi finally said. "I think it wants to kill me."

Hesitantly, Judi talked about her fears, eventually telling the counselor the whole story. When she had finished, she felt drained and sank back into her chair.

Mrs. Abrahams said nothing for a long time. But that was okay. It meant that she was thinking about what Judi had told her.

Finally, the counselor spoke. "Do you have any explanation for all this, Judi?" she asked.

Judi frowned. "Well, either someone is managing to get into Mr. Pascal's locked cabinet, or else—"

"Or else what?"

"Or else the computer has some . . . some supernatural powers." Judi looked up at Mrs. Abrahams to see how she would take this. The counselor didn't seem shocked. She was calm and matter-of-fact.

"Do you believe in the supernatural?" she asked Judi.

"I never thought about it much until this started happening," Judi told her.

Mrs. Abrahams raised a quizzical eyebrow. "You like to read ghost stories, don't you?"

Judi nodded.

"And I'll bet you enjoy horror movies, too."

Judi suddenly felt defensive. "Everybody does."

"But everybody doesn't believe computers are trying to kill them."

Judi sat up. "You don't believe a word I've said!"

"I believe that you believe it," Mrs. Abrahams murmured softly. "Please settle down, Judi. I want to help you. Truly I do."

Judi sat back in her chair.

"The only way you can help me," Judi said, "is to find out how the computer can keep on changing my story."

"Are you sure it's the computer that's changing the story?" Mrs. Abraham's voice was gentle, but her meaning was clear.

"You think I'm writing it myself, don't you?" said Judi accusingly. "You're just like Mr. Pascal. You think I'm just trying to get attention!"

Mrs. Abrahams got up and perched on the edge of her desk. She took Judi's hand and patted it sympathetically.

"I don't know," she said softly. "That's something we need to talk about." She let go of Judi's hand and took an appointment book off her desk. "Let's see." She riffled through the pages. "I think we should begin meeting twice a week."

"Wait," Judi said. "I can prove that I'm telling the truth." Luckily, Judi had brought her books with her. She rummaged through her notebook.

"See!" She thrust a piece of paper at the counselor. "This proves that I'm not lying."

Mrs. Abrahams examined the paper. Then she handed it back to Judi, a question in her eyes. "Are these a few lines from your story?"

Judi nodded. "I wrote that on Tuesday right after class. Those were the last words I entered in the computer."

Mrs. Abrahams face was blank. She seemed at a loss for words. "You write very nicely," she finally said.

Judi tried to explain. "Those were the *last* words I wrote. But the next day, there were new lines added."

The psychologist smiled pleasantly and picked up her appointment book. "That sounds like something we can discuss at our next meeting."

Judi got up. She was disappointed and

should have known better. Even the evidence on the paper hadn't convinced Mrs. Abrahams. She probably thought that Judi had written it just to make her story more believable.

Mrs. Abrahams looked intently at her date book. "I see that you have study hall at 1:30 next Tuesday. I'll put you down for that time. Is that okay with you?"

As if I have a choice, Judi thought. She wanted to tell Mrs. Abrahams that it wasn't okay with her, that it wouldn't do any good. But one way or another, she'd have to go.

Judi sighed and nodded yes.

Mrs. Abrahams rose and walked Judi to the door. "You'll see, Judi, we'll talk this out and soon you'll realize there's nothing to worry about." She walked Judi to the door and smiled encouragingly. "See you in a few days," she said brightly.

With the door safely shut behind her, Judi felt like screaming. But that would only confirm the general opinion that she was weird. Now it was more important than ever to find out what was really happening with her computer. She had to prove that she wasn't making it all up—that she wasn't crazy.

Later, Judi told Shannon what had happened. They were sitting on the stone steps outside school waiting for Judi's mom to pick them up for their shopping expedition.

Shannon stared at her. "You're seeing the school counselor? A psychologist?" she exclaimed. "That's the dumbest thing I ever heard. You're the most normal person I know."

Judi smiled gratefully. Shannon's confidence was exactly what she needed. "I suppose that they've got me down in their records now as a disturbed child," she said, sighing.

Shannon rolled her eyes. "Well, if you're disturbed, then I must be a raving lunatic."

"I guess you are," said Judi.

"Then we're the two crazies." Shannon stuck her fingers into her mouth, pulled it into a grotesque shape and twisted her face. "But," she added as she composed her features, "at least these two crazies are going to the dance."

"What time does it begin?" Judi asked. She tried to move aside as a group of students stomped noisily down the steps. But someone bumped into her and sent her social studies book flying.

"Sorry," mocked Jeff Chapman. He had a huge grin on his face as he swept up the book and handed it to Judi with a bow.

It was hard not to laugh—he looked so funny. Judi forced herself to frown. "Get lost," she told him. The girls watched him running to catch up with his friends.

Shannon nodded solemnly. "I knew it. He likes you."

"That's ridiculous."

"Oh yeah? Then how come he bumped into you?"

Judi didn't have an answer. Anyway, she had too many other things on her mind to even think about Jeff. The computer. Mrs. Abrahams. The dance.

The dance!

Judi suddenly had some new ideas about the dance—and maybe a solution to the mystery of the computer.

"You didn't answer my question, Shannon."

"What question?" asked Shannon.

"What time is the dance?" Judi asked again.

"At seven. The guys are picking us up at 6:45. Jimmy's dad is driving us all there."

"Seven, huh?" Judi made a mental note.

"Yeah. Won't it be fun?"

Judi jumped up. "Fun? It's going to be a lot more than that!"

Shannon looked up in surprise. "What do you mean?"

"I've got a plan!" Judi said. "I know how we can prove that I've been telling the truth about that computer."

Seven

JUDI didn't say anything about her plan right away. She wanted it clear in her own mind before she explained it to Shannon. And luckily, before Shannon could wheedle it out of her, Mrs. Newman drove up to take them shopping. Shannon quickly switched gears to the upcoming dance.

Judi couldn't help getting caught up in the thrill of shopping for the dance. She found a yellow print dress with a scoop neckline that she liked even better than the white one she had in mind. It set off her dark eyes and curly brown hair, and fit her perfectly. Shannon picked out a pale blue dress with a skirt that swirled gracefully. Then they picked out shoes and purses. When they got home it was almost dinnertime.

Shannon stayed to eat. Before dinner, the girls took their boxes up to Judi's room and tried on their dresses again.

"Jimmy's going to love me in this!" said Shannon, twirling around. She paused and began to tug at the neckline. "Maybe I can make this lower."

"You do and your mom will kill you." Judi was admiring herself in the full-length mirror that hung on the inside of her closet door. "I hope Jeff likes this dress," she murmured dreamily.

Shannon turned to Judi. "Jeff! You mean Tom, don't you?"

Judi felt her cheeks grow warm and hoped she wasn't blushing. "Right. Tom."

Shannon shook her head. "I was positive Jeff would ask you to the dance, and I'm hardly ever wrong."

Judi shrugged. "I don't care who I go with. Tom will be just fine."

Shannon was in front of the mirror now, trying to decide on a hair style. "I'll bet Jeff wanted to ask you, but was too shy."

Judi snorted. "Jeff? Shy? He's the biggest clown in school."

"Yeah," said Shannon, pulling some curls down over her forehead. "But he's shy about girls. That's why he's going to the dance alone."

"Jeff will be at the dance?" Judi stared at her friend. She wondered how Shannon always knew what was going on at school

"A whole bunch of guys will be there alone. A lot of the girls, too." Shannon reached back to unzip her dress. "I think it's better to be going with someone." She grinned. "Like us."

Judi nodded, but she wasn't so sure she agreed. Would she have gone alone if she had known Jeff Chapman was going to be there? Oh well, it didn't matter. She didn't even like Jeff.

The girls changed back into their regular clothes and hung their new dresses carefully on padded hangers. Judi walked over to her closet to put the dress away. When she was opened the closet door, she heard a rustling sound, as though something was hiding inside. A wave of fear shot through her and she dropped the dress, hanger and all.

"What's the matter?" Shannon came over.

Judi picked up the dress, smoothed the skirt and examined it carefully to make sure it hadn't gotten dirty. She was still shaking. "I don't know. I heard a noise in the closet, and I was afraid that someone was there."

"In the closet?"

Judi nodded.

Shannon flung the door open all the way and poked through the closet. "There's nothing here except your clothes."

Judi cautiously reached inside and hung up her dress. "It's that computer," she said. "It's got me so edgy that the least little thing makes me panic."

Shannon shook her head. "You scared me. Your face was white. Arc you okay?"

"No," Judi said truthfully. "I won't be okay until I find out what's going on with that stupid computer."

"That reminds me," said Shannon. "What's this plan you were going to tell me about?"

Judi took a deep breath. "It has to do with the dance."

"The dance?" Shannon sprawled on Judi's bed and cupped her chin in her hand. She waited expectantly.

"That's right." Judi sat on the edge of the bed and fiddled with the quilting stitches on the bedspread. Then she looked straight into Shannon's eyes.

"First, you have to swear not to tell a soul," Judi said.

Shannon didn't hesitate. "I swear it. Have I ever let you down?"

Judi shook her head. "No. That's why you're the only one I can trust."

"So tell me," urged Shannon. "What are you going to do on the night of the dance?"

Judi smiled, hugging her secret to herself one last time before sharing it. "Not me," she told her friend. "We. You and I together."

"Wow!" Shannon jumped up and sat cross-legged, staring at Judi. "Tell! Tell!"

Unfortunately, Mrs. Newman chose that very moment to call them to dinner. Shannon pouted at the interruption, but led the charge down the stairs. The main topic of dinner conversation was, of course, the dance. For Patrick, this was about as interesting as a lecture on economics. Finally he banged his spoon and yelled, "No more dance! No more dwesses!"

Shannon's dad came to pick her up before they had finished dessert.

"I'll tell you about my plan tomorrow," Judi whispered as Shannon got her things together.

"You'd better. The dance is coming up soon," Shannon pointed out.

* * * * *

The next day, computer class went badly even though Judi had thought of a new approach the day before. She deleted her own name from the story everywhere it appeared and substituted the name Susan. She figured she couldn't be frightened if a character named Susan was threatened.

But when her story flashed onto the screen that morning, every Susan was changed back to Judi.

Judi was desperate. She started typing almost blindly: *LEAVE ME ALONE! LEAVE ME ALONE!*

Over and over again, she typed *LEAVE ME ALONE!* By the end of the period, she had pages of the stuff and was glad that Mr. Pascal didn't look at her monitor. He'd have hustled her to Mrs. Abrahams' office right away.

After school, Judi walked past the computer room on the way to her locker. She heard voices inside. The door was open a crack, so she looked in.

Mr. Pascal was at his desk shuffling papers. "I have to leave in a few minutes," he was saying. "Will you be able to manage on your own?"

"Sure." It was a guy's voice that answered.

Judi pushed the door open just a bit more. She didn't want Mr. Pascal to catch her spying. He had enough against her already. Trying to keep out of sight, she peered in.

Jimmy Bannister was working at a computer in the back. Judi stared at him. Why was he here after school? And how come the teacher was letting him stay on alone?

Jimmy Bannister! Was he the one?

Just then, Mr. Pascal looked in her direction. Judi ducked back and ran all the way to her locker. She didn't think he had spotted her.

When she met Shannon outside later, Judi told her what she'd seen and what she suspected.

"Jimmy?" Shannon said. "You've got to be kidding! It's not Jimmy. That I can guarantee."

Judi wasn't so sure. Then Shannon pleaded with her to "Tell! Tell!" what she had been hinting about since the day before. Judi laid out her plans for the dance.

"At the dance?" Shannon asked incredulously after Judi explained. "Why do we have to do it during the dance?"

"Don't you see?" Judi's tone was urgent. "If someone is getting into my computer, he or she must be doing it at night when no one is around. The custodians are here until six, and they'd notice anyone sneaking into the computer room. So whoever it is has to be coming into the building after the custodians leave."

"And just who is this someone?"

"That's what we're going to find out," Judi said firmly. "We're going to sneak away from the gym during the dance and watch the computer room."

"That's impossible." Shannon look unconvinced. "People will notice we're gone if we stay away a long time."

"Not if we go one at a time," Judi told her. "Listen, I've thought it all out. We can take turns pretending to go to the ladies' room. Instead, one of us will hang out at the computer room for fifteen minutes or so, then come back, and the other one will go."

"I don't know." Shannon seemed less confident than usual. "What if there's some weird person, or even . . . a ghost?"

"Listen," Judi said, "you don't have to do this. I understand. Really, I do. I can do it myself."

Shannon looked straight into Judi's eyes. "Okay. So I'm scared. Really scared. But I won't let my best friend do this alone."

"It could be risky," Judi said.

"Nah," Shannon said, brushing aside Judi's warning. "Actually, it'll be the most awesome thing I've ever done."

Judi could tell that Shannon was starting to enjoy the idea of an adventure.

"The way I figure it," Shannon explained, "whoever's doing this is either a kid or—or some sort of spook. A really weird spook that's into computers."

"And together," Judi said as she gave Shannon's arm a squeeze, "that's just what we're going to find out."

Eight

THE morning of the dance was gray and rainy. At Judi's school, an assembly was called for the seventh graders. Most of them had never been to a dance before, so the principal talked about how she expected everybody to behave that evening.

It was boring, but the assembly was during Judi's computer period. Judi's spirits rose at the thought of one computer-free day. But then the principal said that periods would be shorter so that no classes would be missed.

Once she was back in computer class, Judi booted up her disk and watched her story appear on the screen. She expected to find all her LEAVE ME ALONE's gone. They were still there, but something had been added at the bottom: *I will not leave you alone! I will get you! I have sharpened my knives, and I am waiting.*

Judi stared at the screen in horror. The thing, or whatever it was, wasn't content just to change Judi's stories. Now it threatened her directly.

Judi quickly thought about showing the screen to Mr. Pascal. Maybe if she tried to explain one more time. . . . He *was* a computer expert. But Judi remembered what happened the last time she looked to him for help and decided not to say anything.

A moment later, Judi found something under her computer. She'd put a pencil down and then couldn't find it. She looked all around the desk and felt underneath the front of the computer. There was a narrow space between the table and the machine. She felt something small and round and pulled it out to look at it.

It was a dark blue button. Torn blue threads clung to the two holes in the middle, as if it had been ripped off a piece of clothing. It looked like it came from a man's jacket.

Judi knew Mr. Pascal often wore a dark blue jacket. She was sure he'd worn one the day before. She looked up slowly. Sure enough, he had on the same blue jacket again. Mr. Pascal was looking down as he thumbed through papers on his desk, so Judi was able to watch him without being noticed. Judi stared intently at his sleeves.

There was a ragged spot on one sleeve. It looked like a button had been torn off. Judi glanced at the button in her hand. There was no doubt about it. The button was from Mr. Pascal's jacket.

Judi wracked her brain. Could Mr. Pascal be the "evil spirit" haunting her computer? No way! It didn't make any sense. No teacher would do such a thing.

But the button told a different story.

Judi grabbed Shannon in the hall after class and told her everything.

Shannon grinned. "You've got to be kidding."

"Oh yeah?" Judi held out the button.

The smile on Shannon's face vanished. "You found that under your computer?"

Judi nodded.

Shannon shook her head. "I know that Mr. Pascal is kind of strange, and can be strict, too. But why would he do a weird thing like this?"

"I don't know," Judi admitted. "Maybe he really *is* crazy."

"Could this button have gotten under your computer some other way?" Shannon asked.

"How?" Judi demanded. "It was on Mr. Pascal's jacket yesterday and today it's under my computer. So how could it have gotten there?"

"Because Mr. Pascal was fiddling with your computer?"

Judi nodded.

"I guess that button tells the whole story," Shannon admitted. "It makes sense. Mr. Pascal is the only one who has a key to the locked disk cabinet." She looked at Judi. "Are you going to tell anyone else?"

"No way! Who'd believe me?" Judi said.

"I guess you're right," Shannon agreed. "Besides, what difference does it make? You know the truth now, and you don't have to be scared any more."

Judi looked at her friend gratefully. Shannon was right. There was nothing to be scared of now. Except Mr. Pascal. And he couldn't scare her now that she knew it was all just a sick joke.

"I should have realized it wasn't the

computer," Judi said, breathing a sigh of relief. "My dad told me that computers can only do what they're programmed to do."

"Now we can concentrate on having fun at the dance tonight and not worry about your stupid computer." Sharon tugged on Judi's arm. "Let's get going. We're late to our next class."

"Judi!"

They stopped short. Judi turned around. It was Mr. Pascal. He stood in the doorway of his classroom and waved to her.

"He wants me to go back," Judi said in a tight voice.

"Go ahead. I'll watch from here to make sure he doesn't try anything weird," Shannon muttered.

"Thanks." Reluctantly, Judi walked back to the computer room.

"Come in for a minute, Judi," Mr. Pascal said. "I want to talk to you."

Nine

MR. Pascal closed the door.

Judi shivered and stared at the floor. She couldn't bear to look at Mr. Pascal, knowing what she knew.

"Judi, I wanted to tell you that yesterday after school I spent some time going over the computers."

"Yesterday?" Judi looked up reluctantly. Mr. Pascal's face was calm.

He nodded. "I took particular pains with your computer."

"You did?"

"You seem to be having so much difficulty with it. I went over everything that could possibly cause a problem."

Judi tightened her fist around the button.

"There's nothing wrong with that computer, Judi. I can guarantee it." He held up his arm and pointed to the empty spot on his sleeve. "Look. I took that computer apart so thoroughly that I even lost a button in the process." Mr. Pascal smiled. He actually smiled! "Now, if your computer malfunctions we can chalk it up to a button in the works."

Judi held out her own hand. "Here's your button, Mr. Pascal. It was on my desk."

He took it with a look of pleasure. "Thank you, Judi. Now remember, there's nothing to cause you problems with that computer."

He was still smiling. Judi was stunned.

"Thanks for looking at the computer, Mr. Pascal," she said tonelessly, and walked out.

Judi wondered if Mr. Pascal was telling the truth. Maybe he noticed that he was missing a button and made up a story about checking the computer. Tom or Jimmy or one of the other guys might be playing a joke on her, but no one had a key to the disk cabinet except Mr. Pascal. But that was crazy, wasn't it?

When Judi came out of the computer room, Shannon took one look at her and said, "Uh-oh!"

"It's not Mr. Pascal." Judi stopped short.

He seemed normal enough, but was there something phony about the way he smiled? "At least," Judi added, "I'm not sure. We'll have to find out at the dance."

The dance, Judi thought. She'd solve the riddle tonight at the dance. Time was running out—the threats on her monitor were getting worse.

Mr. Pascal? One of the guys? The computer itself? Could one of them want to hurt her? There just had to be a logical solution she hadn't thought of yet. Judi rubbed her forehead. Her head was pounding.

She'd find out the truth tonight. She just had to!

Ten

GETTING dressed for the party was no fun. Outside, the rain had stopped and the sky had cleared, but inside, Judi was feeling as dreary as the day had been.

While she showered, Judi had a terrifying vision of a long, sharp knife ripping through the shower curtain. When she laid out her clothes, she imagined a dark stream of blood slithering down her soft yellow dress. She realized that it was only a shadow, but the scary feeling stayed with her.

Judi's mother came in to help. "Your first dance!" Mrs. Newman sighed as she carefully inspected Judi's dress spread out on the bed. She nodded her approval, and then came to stand behind Judi, who was curling her hair.

Judi's face, reflected in the mirror, was pale. "Aren't you excited, Judi?" Mrs. Newman asked.

Judi shrugged and put another lock of hair in her curling iron.

Mrs. Newman watched her daughter closely. "Are you all right, Judi?"

Judi nodded and said nothing.

Mrs. Newman took the curling iron from Judi. "I'll get this spot in back," she offered. Judi watched in the mirror as her mother quickly finished the job.

"There!" Judi's mom stood back to admire the result. "Your hair looks lovely, Judi."

Judi sighed and slipped into her dress. Mrs. Newman zipped up the back while Judi struggled with the small pearl buttons at the wrists.

"Aren't you happy about the dance?" Mrs. Newman asked.

"Sure I am." Even to Judi, her voice sounded unconvincing.

"Don't you like the boy you're going with?"

"He's okay," Judi said, pouting. She wished her mom would stop probing.

"You could have gone alone. I hear that lots of kids are doing just that."

An image of Jeff Chapman briefly crossed

Judi's mind. She wondered if he'd joke around at the dance. Maybe not. The principal made it clear that anyone who acted up would be kicked out.

"Tom's a good guy," Judi told her mother. "I don't mind going with him."

But Judi wondered. *Was* Tom a good guy? What did she know about him, after all? And what about Jimmy or Jeff? Either of them could be playing a sick trick on her. And then there was Mr. Pascal, weird as he was. Or was it the computer itself threatening her?

Soon Judi would know the answer.

Mrs. Newman's voice broke into Judi's thoughts. "I just wish you seemed happier. You look beautiful." She led Judi to the full-length mirror. Judi gazed at her reflection. The girl in the glass did look pretty. But Judi had the eerie feeling that it was someone else staring back, not her at all.

Judi felt a little better when Jimmy's dad drove up in the car. Judi was the last one to be picked up. The others were already in the car. Shannon was beautiful in blue. Her gleaming hair waved softly around her face, and her eyes sparkled. The guys looked kind of grown-up in jackets and ties—different from the way they usually looked in school. Then Jimmy and Tom started punching each other, and they seemed more like the seventh graders Judi knew. Judi felt comforted.

The theme of the dance was spring, and the school gym was transformed with festive ribbons, hangings, posters, and balloons. Bright paper daffodils, tulips, and hyacinths sprouted along the walls in shades of yellow, red, and green. Colorful paper flowers brightened the platform where the band was playing.

Most of the kids had come by themselves or with friends. They stood in tight little knots, groups of girls and groups of guys, waiting for someone to break the ice. Most of the guys crowded around the refreshment tables. Judi's group headed straight for the goodies.

One of the girls standing nearby was in Judi's computer class. When she spotted Judi, she smirked.

"Did your computer write any good stories today, Judi?"

The girls she was with all giggled loudly. Judi glared at them and grabbed a cup of punch. While she was sipping the pink liquid, her eyes strayed to a door at the far end of the room. That door opened to the hall Judi would have to go down to reach the computer room. Judi pulled Shannon away from the crowd. She pointed to the exit and whispered, "Do you want to go first, or should I?"

Shannon groaned. "But we just got here!"

Judi nodded. "I'll go first."

She excused herself and headed toward the rear of the gym. Judi felt a tingle of excitement mixed with fear. She was almost at the door when someone yanked her hair. She spun around.

Jeff Chapman stood there smiling innocently, but he had a twinkle in his eye. "It wasn't me," he declared.

"I'll bet!" Judi gave him an icy look and continued on her way. She had a more serious problem to deal with. Reaching the exit, she looked around hastily to see if anyone had noticed her. Everyone was busy trying to be noticed by others. Only Jimmy Bannister, talking to Shannon on the other side of the room, suddenly looked in Judi's direction.

Jimmy, the computer whiz!

Judi blinked. When she looked again, a large group of kids had moved to the center of the room and blocked her view of Jimmy. Judi rubbed her eyes. This is ridiculous, she thought. He probably wasn't even looking at me. Well, she'd know soon!

The doorway she went through also led to the bathrooms, so no one would suspect that she was going somewhere else. Once past the ladies' room, she hurried to the end of the hall and quickly turned the corner into the next corridor. Here, she breathed more easily. No one would see her now. The computer room was at the end of the hall.

Judi hesitated. The school building was so different at night, with long, deserted corridors and darkened classrooms eerily silent. Judi forced herself to keep moving until she was in front of the computer classroom door.

Judi half-hoped the door would be locked. If it was, it'd be the end of her plan and she could go enjoy the dance. Judi looked quickly in both directions and put her hand on the doorknob. The knob turned easily. Judi hesitated once more, then quickly opened the door and slipped inside.

The computers gleamed softly in the darkened room, reflecting the dim light cast from the corridor. Once she closed the door, Judi knew that it would be difficult to see.

She looked around to figure out the best place to hide.

If she stood in the corner behind the last row of computers, she could see who might come through the door without being seen herself. She took a deep breath, pulled the door shut behind her, and plunged the room into darkness. Then she carefully felt her way to the back.

Judi didn't know how long she waited there. It was too dark to see the face of her wristwatch. Even worse than the stillness was the occasional creaking and knocking of the building's pipes. The noises were followed by silence again.

And the shadows! The darkened room was filled with even darker shadows. As Judi stared, the shadows moved and shifted and took on new shapes. Sometimes the shapes came toward her, but then—nothing.

With relief, Judi decided she shouldn't stay away from the dance too long—her friends might send someone to look for her. Judi stumbled to the door and was glad to leave the creepy room behind.

Glancing at her watch, Judi realized she'd been gone twenty minutes. She took a deep breath and threaded her way through the crowd to look for Shannon and Tom. Kids were dancing now, and everybody seemed more relaxed. Everybody except Judi. She felt like an outsider

Finally, Judi spotted Shannon and Jimmy dancing near the refreshment table. She caught Shannon's eye and nodded. That was the signal that it was Shannon's turn to stand watch in the computer room. Shannon smiled in acknowledgment. Judi watched Shannon say something to Jimmy, stop dancing, and slip out the rear exit.

"Where have you been, Judi?" Judi turned around, startled. It was Tom. "I've been looking for you to dance."

Was he really looking for her to dance, Judi wondered. Or did he want to know if the coast was clear to sneak into the computer room? It was awful suspecting everyone.

"I've been looking for you, too," Judi said quickly. "It's so crowded here, it's hard to find anyone." She managed to sound like she'd been there for a long time searching for her date in the crowd.

Judi and Tom found an empty spot on the dance floor. Judi danced, but her mind was elsewhere. She imagined Shannon in the computer room. What if someone came in? Would Shannon know what to do? Judi felt a pang of fright. What if she'd sent her friend into danger?

Judi was too wrapped up to be aware of what was going on around her, but she did notice that Tom was a terrible dancer. He had no sense of rhythm at all. Any other time, it would have been funny. Now it was just another problem to deal with.

She saw Jeff Chapman lounging with his buddies across the room. He turned his back when he saw her glance at him, but Judi knew that he'd been looking at her. She wondered if Shannon was right when she said that Jeff was always staring at her.

And where was Jimmy Bannister? Judi didn't see him anywhere.

Judi gave Tom an encouraging smile, then glanced toward the exit. Suddenly, Shannon appeared. Judi glanced at her watch. Shannon had only been gone ten minutes. She looked at Shannon again. She was standing stock still just inside the door. Her face was a ghastly shade of gray.

Shannon looked like she'd seen a ghost!

97

Eleven

"WHAT happened?" Judi hissed once she was at Shannon's side. She had escaped from Tom with an excuse about having to fix her shoe.

Shannon trembled and declared, "I'm not going back there again! That room is spooky! There are all kinds of shadows and scary noises."

Judi felt a mixture of relief and disappointment. Nothing important had happened. Shannon had only experienced the same things Judi had.

"The same thing happened to me," she told Shannon. "But it was just the pipes and some shadows."

"I don't care!" Shannon said obstinately. "I won't go in there again!"

Judi sighed. "I guess I'll have to do it myself."

Shannon grabbed her arm. "Judi, this is dumb. No one is going to be in that room tonight except us."

Judi felt betrayed. "Are you saying that the whole thing is my imagination? I thought that you believed me."

Shannon shook her head. "I still believe you, Judi. I just don't think that this standing guard plan is going to work."

"But don't you see," Judi pleaded. "It's the only way I can prove I'm not making it up. Please, Shannon, help me."

Shannon's face softened. She sighed. "Okay, Judi, I'll help you. But I won't go back there alone. And I won't let you go alone either. That room is spooky. There's something there that scares me. It doesn't feel safe."

"How about if we go together," Judi suggested.

"Okay," Shannon agreed. "I'll do it, but I won't like it."

Judi bit her lip. "What should we tell the guys? It'll look funny if we both disappear."

"Forget them! They'll never even notice." Shannon snorted. "Look!" She pointed to the dance floor. Both Jimmy and Tom were dancing with other girls.

Judi didn't care who Tom was with. At least if he was dancing, he wasn't in the computer room. But she could see that Shannon was upset. This was a perfect time to get her away.

"Let's go now," Judi whispered.

She and Shannon slipped out the door and made their way down the dimly lit, deserted corridors to the computer room. They opened the door and peered inside. The room was just as it was when Judi left earlier: empty except for the gleaming computers and the dark shadows shifting in the corners.

"Let's hide behind the back row," whispered Judi. They closed the door, once more plunging the room into darkness, and made their way to the rear. They waited, standing close together.

In the silence, Judi swore she could hear the beating of their hearts. A loud creaking sound came from the other side of the room. Shannon gripped Judi's arm so tightly that it hurt.

"It's only the pipes," Judi assured her in a whisper. Shannon glanced up at the pipes in the ceiling, and Judi felt the pressure on her arm decrease.

Judi relaxed just a bit. The weird shadows were still all around them, but it didn't seem as scary now that Shannon was with her. Whenever there was a sudden movement or sound, it helped to have another person to grab onto.

Then, just when Judi felt calmer, she heard a sudden noise.

The doorknob was turning! Shannon gasped and clutched Judi's arm in a painful grip. Light from the hall filtered in, sending the shadows dancing into the far corners of the room. Slowly, the door opened.

This was the moment Judi had been waiting for, but she hadn't planned on her reaction. She'd never known such bone-chilling terror. Her mouth was dry. She wanted to scream, but no sound came out of her tight, parched throat. She felt Shannon trembling beside her, too.

Quickly, Judi pulled Shannon down to crouch behind the rear computers. The girls held on to each other tightly.

A figure appeared in the entrance, but the door closed again too quickly for them to make out who, or what, it was. Darkness once more enveloped the room. Judi was just able to make out the shadowy figure moving stealthily across the front of the room.

At least it wasn't coming toward them.

The intruder stopped at the filing cabinet. There was a click, then a groaning sound as one of the drawers opened. Judi peered through the darkness as the figure moved toward the teacher's desk and put a box on it.

Judi drew in her breath sharply. The box. It had to be the one where the data disks were kept.

The sound of a key being inserted into a lock came next. Judi nudged Shannon to be sure she noticed, too. This was no ghost. This was a real, live person. Someone who had managed to obtain keys to the file cabinet and the disk box.

The figure took something out of the box, moved to a computer in the front row, and sat down. A flashlight switched on. It gave just enough light for whoever was there to be able to operate the computer. A whirring noise told Judi that the computer had been turned on. After a short pause, Judi could hear the tapping of the keys.

This was it. Judi knew that she had to act now. She poked Shannon and held up her hand to signal that Shannon should stay where she was. Then, with all the stealth she could muster, Judi crept toward the front of the room. She hid behind computers, desks, cabinets, anything that would shield her. She watched the figure at the computer, absorbed in its task. Slowly, silently, Judi edged her way toward the light switch near the door. Closer and closer she crept.

Suddenly, the figure at the computer looked up. Judi stood stock still, flattened against the wall. She could hardly breathe. Somehow, she got through the dangerous moment. The intruder at the computer seemed satisfied that no one else was present, and bent down to work once more. *Click, click, click* went the keys.

Changing my story, and trying to scare the living daylights out of me, Judi thought. Her anger melted some of her terror. Now is the time, Judi decided, with a surge of excitement.

Carefully, Judi sidled along the wall. She knew just about where the light switch was on the wall close to the door. She hoped she was right. She reached the door, and, holding her breath, moved one hand up along the wall.

Then she felt it. The switch. Her fingers curled around the square piece of metal. She hesitated for a moment. Who was she going to see seated at her desk? Judi swallowed hard. Then, with a determined motion, she pushed up the switch.

The room was instantly flooded with light. Shannon stood up from her hiding place. Judi looked triumphantly at the figure now staring open-mouthed at her from the computer.

Twelve

THE boy looked startled. Then his mouth spread into a slow, crooked grin. "Hi, Judi," he said.

"Jeff Chapman!"

Shannon, who had come running down to the front of the room when the lights went on, was more blunt.

"Jeff, you creep!" she said.

Jeff held up his hands in surrender. "I guess you got me." His voice teetered on the edge of laughter.

Judi's fear exploded into anger. Jeff's total lack of embarrassment really ticked her off.

"You jerk!" she shouted. "You rotten jerk! How could you do this to me?" Blind with fury, she walked over to the desk and punched Jeff hard on his arm.

Jeff stood up. He touched his arm gingerly. "Hey! I don't know why you're acting this way."

"Because she was scared to death!" screeched Shannon. "Wouldn't you be frightened if you thought that someone was trying to kill you?"

Jeff shuffled uncomfortably and looked away. "I mean—it was just a joke. I didn't know you'd take it like this."

Judi could hardly control herself. "How did you think I'd take it?" she demanded. "Everyone thought I was going crazy, including me. They were even making me see a psychologist. And all because of you!"

Jeff's eyes widened. "Really? I didn't know about that. Honestly, I never meant it to go that far."

"What *did* you mean, jerk?" demanded Shannon.

"I just wanted to scare Judi a little, that's all." The easy grin had left his face now. He hung his head. "I'm sorry, Judi. Really I am."

"I don't believe you," Judi told him accusingly. "I think you're laughing at me right now, just the way you always do when you play one of your stupid jokes."

"Well," he admitted, "it did seem funny. I thought you'd figure out what was happening before this, though."

Judi shook her head. "Why me?" she demanded. "Why pick on me? What did I ever do to you?"

Jeff blushed. "I dunno." He shrugged. "I guess I just wanted to get to know you better. Then I got hold of the keys. I picked your disk because I was curious to know what you were writing."

"The keys?" The girls stared at him.

"Yeah. Mr. Pascal had an extra set in his desk. I was working in the computer room one day after school. Mr. Pascal had to leave. He gave me his extra keys so I could lock up when I was finished. He never asked for them back." Jeff shrugged. "He must have forgotten that he gave them to me. I guess he never uses them and didn't notice they were gone."

"So you just *kept* them?" Judi rolled her eyes in disbelief.

Jeff nodded. "I didn't know what I was going to use them for," he said. "I just figured that they might come in handy for a good joke sometime."

"Oh yeah! Some joke!" Shannon said sarcastically.

"Anyway," he continued, "I opened the box of disks from our class, and . . . " He reddened again. "And I looked at yours, Judi, just to see what you had written."

"And then you saw it was a ghost story," prompted Judi.

Jeff nodded. "At first, I only planned to change your story that one time," he said. "I mean, it wasn't easy to keep sneaking back into the classroom after hours." He couldn't hold back a grin. "I figured you'd have a good laugh over it, then I'd tell you how I did it, and . . . well, I guess I hoped you'd be impressed." Jeff had gotten up now. He paced the room as if he were looking for an escape.

"And then Mr. Pascal made a big fuss in class, and you were so upset. I guess it seemed like a good joke to keep it up for a while," he concluded lamely. "Actually, I was going to tell you about it tonight."

"Tonight?"

"Yeah. At the dance. I figured maybe we'd start talking and—you know. And then you came in with that Tiny Tom character."

"Tom's not the one who's a character," Judi said angrily. "You are!"

Judi couldn't ignore the fact that Jeff

wanted to impress her. But right now, she was too furious to really take it in.

"This was a sick idea!" she added.

That reminded Judi about the disk in her computer. She looked at the monitor. There was a new warning on the screen: *I didn't get you at the dance. But I know where you live. My knife is still ready. Next time you're alone in the house . . .*

Judi shook her head to think how scared she'd have been to see those words on her monitor. "Sick!" she repeated. "Sick! Sick! Sick!"

For a few minutes, they were all silent. No one knew what else to say. Judi stared at the monitor. Shannon glared at Jeff. Jeff looked at the floor.

Finally, Shannon asked, "What are we going to do now?"

Judi faced her tormentor with blazing eyes. "You're going to confess!" she demanded. "You're going to tell Mr. Pascal what you've done."

Jeff raised his head. He turned pale at the mention of Mr. Pascal. "Do I have to?"

Judi nodded firmly. "Monday, at the beginning of school, before homeroom. You're going to go to the computer room and tell Mr. Pascal everything. If you don't, I will!"

"Okay!" Jeff looked miserable.

"And you're going to tell everybody else, too," Judi continued relentlessly. "You're going to tell them right now."

"Not here at the dance?" Jeff protested.

"Yes, right here. Right now!" Judi insisted. "I want everyone to know that you're the weirdo, not me."

"Okay," Jeff agreed. "I'll tell them."

They put the disk away and locked the box and cabinet. Judi insisted on holding on to the keys until she could return them to Mr. Pascal. "I don't trust you," she told Jeff. "Not one bit!"

They turned off the lights and left. Before closing the door, Judi looked back into the room. The dark shadows that had terrified her only a short time ago now looked exactly like what they were—harmless shadows, nothing more. It was just an ordinary school classroom.

Judi didn't really believe that Jeff would keep his word, but he did. Judi watched him talking to groups of people back at the dance. Later, some of the kids went out of their way to be friendly and tell her that they didn't see anything unusual about her recent behavior.

Judi enjoyed the rest of that evening. Relaxed at last, she danced with lots of the guys. Even Jeff asked her to dance. She was shocked he had such nerve, and refused. She was just a bit sorry when she saw how cute he looked, walking away with his hands jammed in his pockets and a frown on his face.

I don't care if he is cute, she told herself, I'll never have anything to do with that jerk!

She wondered what Mr. Pascal would do to him. She hoped that it would be a punishment he'd never forget.

Thirteen

MONDAY morning was bright and sunny, just like Judi's mood. When she brushed her hair, the face looking back at her in the mirror glowed.

"You seem happy today," Mrs. Newman commented at breakfast.

"I sure am!" Judi waited patiently for Patrick to pass the cornflakes. She turned to her father, who was gingerly lifting slices of hot toast out of the toaster. "Dad, you were right about computers."

"I was?"

Judi nodded. "Computers don't have minds of their own. They can only do what's programmed into them."

Her father grinned. "Well, there was never any doubt about that."

"I thought there was," Judi confessed. "But you know all about that, don't you?"

Her parents looked confused. "About what?"

"The stories in the computer."

Judi's mom shook her head. "We have no idea what you're talking about, Judi."

Judi couldn't believe what she was hearing. "I thought Mr. Pascal told you. Or Mrs. Abrahams."

"Only that you might be having a personality conflict with your computer teacher and that it was affecting your work," Mrs. Newman said. "We hoped Mrs. Abrahams could help you deal with it. You never seemed to want to talk about it. We didn't want to nag at you once we knew you were getting help."

Judi sighed. "It wasn't like that at all." She started to tell all the details of the last few days.

"Judi!" her mother exclaimed. "How could you take such a chance, wandering around deserted hallways and hiding in a dark room?"

"A *dawk woom*," Patrick shouted approvingly, and banged his spoon on the table.

Judi shrugged and went on with her story,

finishing triumphantly with her discovery that Jeff Chapman was the culprit.

Mr. Newman frowned. "That kid!" he exclaimed angrily. "If I ever get my hands on him!"

"Don't worry," Judi assured him. "When Jeff tells Mr. Pascal what he did, he's sure to get it."

"Let's hope so!" Mr. Newman's face, which had turned fiery red, returned to its normal color. "Anyway, Judi," he added, "at least you don't think that a computer has any strange powers."

"It's incredible," Mrs. Newman said, shaking her head, "that you could have gone through all this without our knowledge. We thought you just didn't like computers. Or Mr. Pascal. Or both."

"What's a *'puter*?" asked Patrick.

"It's a machine." Judi said firmly. She felt in control again. It felt good. "Just a machine, and nothing more."

* * * * *

The computers were standing at attention later that morning when Judi entered the computer room. Judi stopped at Mr. Pascal's desk to get her disk, and looked at him expectantly. He was looking at some papers spread out on his desk. He glanced up, saw Judi, and turned back without comment.

Judi was disappointed. She took her disk and went to her desk. She wondered about Mr. Pascal's response. It was true that Mr. Pascal was a cool one. He hardly ever demonstrated anything approaching emotion, but after everything that had happened, it seemed like even *he* might show some reaction. Had Jeff gone back on his word? Slipping her disk into the computer, Judi glanced toward Jeff's station at the back of the room.

It was empty!

The creep! He hadn't confessed to the teacher after all. Instead, he stayed home that day. How convenient for him! Furiously, Judi attacked the keys. She was so angry that it wouldn't have surprised her to see steam coming out of her ears.

The little coward, she thought. He couldn't get up the courage to tell the teacher. Just wait until she got her hands on him. She'd make him sorry he was ever born.

The most humiliating thought of all was that she had almost believed him when he said he had done the whole thing just to get to know her better. Judi could have kicked herself for being so gullible. At least she had refused to dance with him, so she didn't feel like a complete fool.

Judi glanced at the monitor idly. She knew what would appear there. She had seen for herself the nonsense that Jeff had written at the end of her story. But what Judi saw on the monitor was completely unexpected:

Dear Judi,

Please accept my apology for my suspicions and lack of belief in your truthfulness. The student responsible has told me everything, and is receiving an appropriate punishment.

Sincerely,
Mr. Pascal

P.S. I have erased everything on your data disk, and hope that you will begin a new story.

Judi looked up to see Mr. Pascal's eyes on her. He gave her a small, rare smile and came up to stand beside her station. "Are you convinced now," he asked, "that computers can't change data all by themselves?"

Judi nodded. "I guess there aren't any ghosts in my computer. It's not programmed for terror, after all."

The teacher cleared his throat. "I'm sorry," he went on, looking a bit uncomfortable, "that I was so quick to judge you harshly." He sighed. "I guess I've been doing a lot of that since my wife died two years ago. I should have been more understanding. I'll know better from now on."

"Thank you." Judi said it with relief and a smile.

Why, he's just lonely and sad, Judi thought. And I was almost ready to think he could be some kind of sicko!

"We'll be using the word processing program only a few more days," Mr. Pascal continued. "But I hope you'll start another story. You write so well and so quickly that you'll probably finish it even with all the time that you've lost."

"I'll get busy on it right now," Judi assured him. She was afraid to ask about Jeff. What punishment did he get? She wondered where

Jeff was. Perhaps he was in the principal's office. Maybe his parents were even being called in.

Now that everyone knew the truth and Judi was in the clear, she felt a twinge of sympathy for Jeff. After all, he came up with the stupid idea because he liked her. In spite of her anger, Judi could feel her cheeks grow warm at the thought. And then an idea came to her for a story. Quickly, she began to tap it out on the keyboard.

It was not a ghost story. No way! This time, she was writing a romantic adventure. It was going to be about a teenager who was willing to risk his life to save the girl he loved. The girl's name was, as usual, Judi. The guy's name was Jeff.

Later, Judi found out what had happened to Jeff Chapman. Shannon told her. The whole school seemed to know about it, except Judi.

"He got in-school suspension," said Shannon, in an awed voice. "For a *whole week.*"

In-school suspension meant that you sat in the principal's office all day doing work assigned by your teachers. A kid on in-school suspension couldn't go to classes, and couldn't even go to the cafeteria, but had to have lunch right there in the office. The only punishment worse than in-school suspension was out-of-school suspension, and a kid had to practically kill someone before that was ever prescribed. It was unusual for anyone to get more than three days of in-school suspension.

Jeff was paying a heavy price for what he had done. But it couldn't be too heavy as far as Judi was concerned. She still got angry every time she thought about it.

A few days later, she had cooled off enough to stop and listen when Jeff came over to her outside after school. Shannon had stepped away for a minute to talk to another girl. Judi stood alone.

"Hi, Judi." Jeff blushed dark red.

Judi didn't answer. But she didn't walk away.

"I'm sorry for what I did, Judi. Really," Jeff stammered.

Judi frowned, but she stayed.

"Could you forgive me?" Jeff pleaded.

"Maybe some day." Jeff seemed so miserable that Judi began to relent. At least a little.

"Did you hear about my suspension?"

Judi nodded.

Jeff dug his heel into the soft earth bordering the walk. "I guess I deserve it."

"Yes," Judi agreed. "You really do deserve it. Still," she added, "a whole week in-school suspension—that's pretty harsh." Judi's anger was beginning to fade. She never could hold a grudge. She and Shannon had gotten into some terrible fights through the years. But they always made up, and usually Judi forgot what made her angry in the first place. She wondered if it would be the same with Jeff.

Jeff managed a lopsided grin. "My dad warned me that my practical jokes would get me into big trouble one day. I guess it finally happened." He looked at Judi steadily at last. "Honestly, I never thought you'd take it so seriously and be so scared."

Judi had never noticed how deep blue Jeff's eyes were. He was tall, too. She had to tilt her head to look at him. A few weeks ago, she would have thought it was heaven to be standing here like this having a heart-to-heart talk with Jeff Chapman. Actually, it felt nice, even now, even after all that had happened. She wondered if he would tell her once more that he was sorry.

If he does, she decided, maybe I'll forgive him.

"I'm really sorry, Judi," he said again, looking at Judi earnestly.

Judi shrugged. "Let's just let it go," she said. Her heart felt lighter than it had in a long time. "Besides," she added, smiling impulsively, "I'll admit something. At times, it was exciting. Scary—but exciting." She noticed Shannon a few feet away staring at her curiously.

"I thought it was funny at the time," Jeff admitted. "But there's nothing hilarious about a week's suspension." He dug his foot further into the ground. Judi wondered how far down it had to go to begin growing roots. Jeff nodded glumly. "I think I've learned a lesson." He held out his hand. "Can we be friends?"

"No more practical jokes?" Judi couldn't resist zinging it to him one more time.

"No." He hesitated. "At least none involving computers."

Judi took his outstretched hand. "Okay. Friends."

Jeff's grip was firm, and his smile was sincere. He said goodbye and walked off down the path. Judi watched him, wondering at the unexpected way things had turned out. Life sure was strange, Judi thought. You could never predict today what might happen tomorrow.

"I told you!" Shannon dashed up and grabbed Judi's arm. "Didn't I always say that Jeff Chapman liked you?"

Judi nodded. "You were right, Shannon. But who ever thought that I'd end up being friends with the ghost in my computer?"

About the Author

Carol H. Behrman was born in Brooklyn, New York, and now lives in Fair Lawn, New Jersey, with her husband, Edward.

Besides teaching writing workshops and speaking at writers' conferences, she has written more than ten novels for children and young adults. She is also the author of several nonfiction books and a writing text for students in grades five through eight.

She has gotten many of her ideas for her novels from the experiences of her children as they were growing up. Other ideas were inspired by students at the middle school in Glen Ridge, New Jersey, where the author taught for many years.

Besides writing, Carol H. Behrman enjoys traveling, crossword puzzles, and reading.

Programmed for Terror is her second book for Willowisp Press.